When Mom Turned into a
MONSTER

Joanna Harrison

Carolrhoda Books, Inc. / Minneapolis

For my Mum,
with lots of love

Copyright © 1996 by Joanna Harrison

This edition first published in 1996 by Carolrhoda Books, Inc.

First published in England in 1996 by HarperCollins Publishers Ltd, London.

Carolrhoda Books, Inc., c/o The Lerner Group
241 First Avenue North, Minneapolis, MN 55401

Library of Congress Cataloging-in-Publication-Data

Harrison, Joanna.
    When mom turned into a monster / by Joanna Harrison.
      p. cm.
    "First published in England in 1996 by HarperCollins
Publishers Ltd."—T.p. verso
    Summary: Instead of helping their mother get ready for
company, Katie and Sam cause one problem after another,
turning their mother into a monster.
    ISBN 1-57505-013-7
    [1. Behavior—Fiction. 2. Mother and child—Fiction.]
I. Title.
PZ7.H252Wh 1996
[E]—dc20   95–43707
                                                   CIP
                                                   AC

Printed in Hong Kong
Bound in the United States of America
1 2 3 4 5 6 – O/S – 01 00 99 98 97 96

We were having breakfast when the phone rang.
"Hello," said Mom. "Hi... yes... yes... five o'clock...
great!... no... no problem... bye." She hung up the phone.

"Aarrgghh!" she cried. "Your cousins are coming over this afternoon.

The house is a mess, and there's nothing to eat."

"Oh, no!" said Sam.

"Children, make your hair and comb your beds,
and do it right!"
"Yes, Mom," we said. We knew what she meant.
She just wasn't really herself.

Mom spent most of the morning cleaning the house.
There was a lot to do...

washing the breakfast dishes... dusting...

vacuuming up the cat hairs...

and scrubbing the toilet.

Sam and I forgot all about making our beds.
We made a jungle camp instead.

We had a great time, but I don't think Mom was very pleased.

Then we all had to go to the supermarket.

Mom started to yell. "Will you two stop fighting!"

When we got there, we wanted some potato chips, but Mom just kept saying no.

She seemed to be getting really mad.

So we told her she was horrible.

After a while, we got so fed up that we went off to do our own shopping. We were just starting to enjoy ourselves when suddenly...

we crashed into some carts. I looked up to
see a man standing over us.
"And WHERE is your mother?" he asked angrily.

"HERE," growled Mom.

Mom wouldn't let us have any candy, so I started to cry.
Sam told me to be quiet because everyone was looking at us...

so I cried even more, and then Sam joined in.

When we got home, Mom unpacked the
groceries while we tried to make a cake.

But we made such a mess that Mom told
us to stay out of her way.

So Sam and I made an obstacle course on the lawn.
It was lots of fun going through it on our bikes.
"I hope Mom won't mind the mud," said Sam.

When it started to rain, we came inside.

Mom had put the food out on the table. It looked so delicious that we just had to help ourselves.

It was only after we'd eaten seven sandwiches, four cupcakes, ten cookies, and most of the chocolate off the top of the cake that we realized Mom might not be too happy with us. So we ran upstairs to hide.

"What a mess!" said Sam, stuffing a half-eaten sandwich into his pocket.

Then we heard footsteps... clomp... clomp... clomp coming up the stairs.

We dived under the covers.

Sam looked at his watch. It was nearly five o'clock.

Suddenly the door burst open. It was Mom. I'd never seen her looking THIS angry before! She tried to shout, but

all that came out was smoke and flames and a terrible roar.
"Oh, no," whispered Sam. "She's gone completely nuts."

But Mom just slumped into a chair.
"I used to be a nice person," she moaned. "But
all your mess and fighting and whining and yelling
has turned me... sob... into... sob... A MONSTER!"

Poor Mom! We didn't know what to say. So we
decided to clean up our room and make the beds.

I made Mom a cup of tea. Then we put away
our coats and boots, and vacuumed the floor.

We put our bikes in the garage...

and made some more sandwiches.

We were just brushing our
hair when Mom came in.

"I'm sorry," she said. "I've been such a monster."
"Oh, Mom," we both cried, "we're sorry too."

And we hugged each other tight.
Suddenly the doorbell rang...

Our cousins had arrived!

As Mom went downstairs to open the door,
we suddenly realized that she still had
monstrous hair!

Luckily we warned her just in time.

Well, we made it.

Aunt Jane seemed impressed.
"Wow!" she said. "Everything looks wonderful.
I hope it wasn't too much trouble."
"Oh, it was nothing," murmured Mom.

At the table, our cousins were awful. They were such monsters they didn't even notice that their mother had grown...

a long... green... tail!